George Pearce

and his
huge massive ears

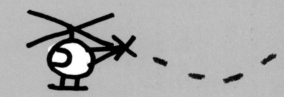

By Felix Massie

Frances Lincoln
Children's Books

This is George Pearce.

Actually, no, wait...

This is George Pearce.

You see...

George has two really remarkable things
either side of his head, that stick out like wings.

Far from being useful for being able to fly,
they allow him to listen to things on the sly.

But the trouble with hearing each word that is said...
Well, soon the words started to fill George's head.

COOOOOOOOOOOOOOOOOOOl!!

Some opinions were good...

While others were bad...

RUUUUUUUUUUUUUUUUbbish!

And that was enough to turn any boy mad.

He'd hear every thought,
every view, every whine
and thought if he listened,
he'd fit in just fine!

He'd spend hours listening—
he'd listen all day long,
while trying his hardest
to sort right from wrong.

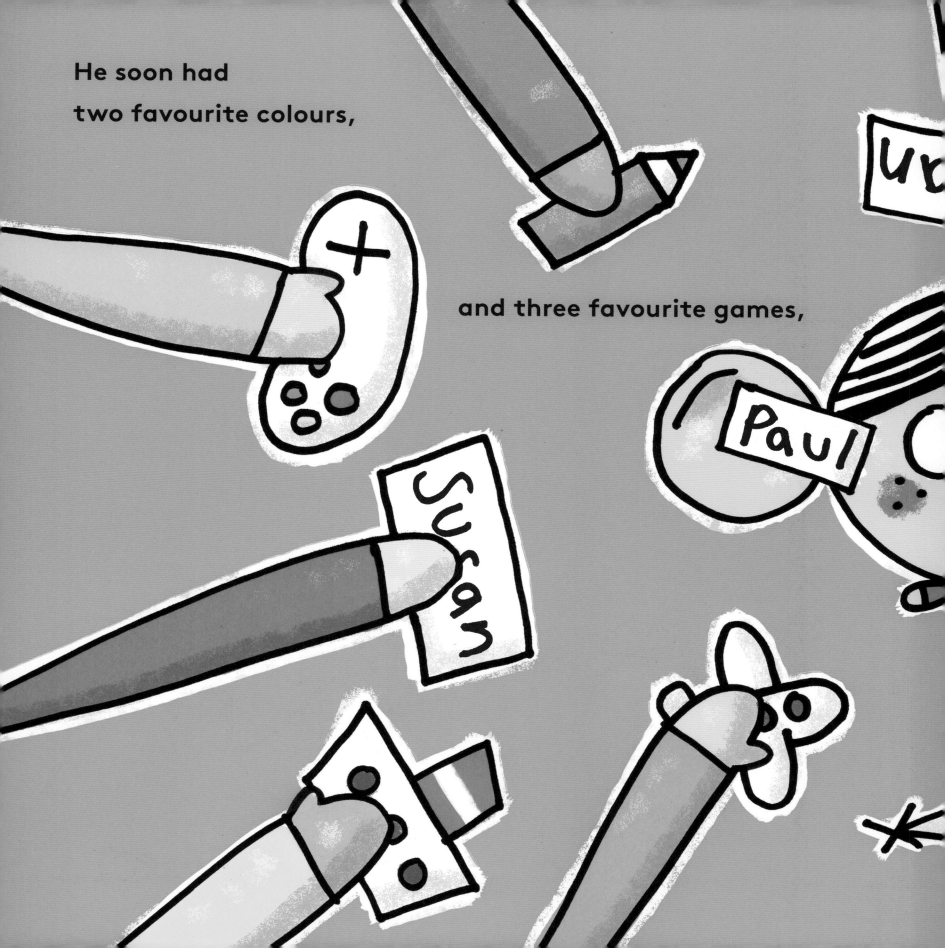

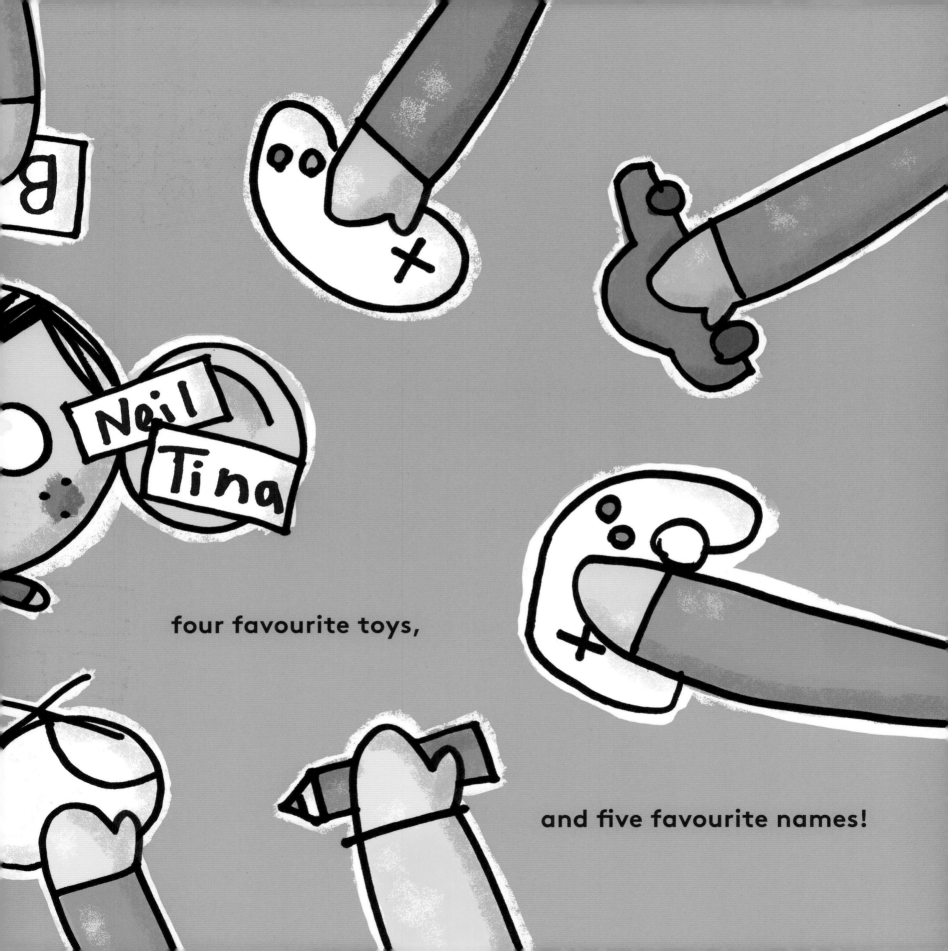

four favourite toys,

and five favourite names!

He tried to keep going, but soon he found out
it's not easy to please everyone with a mouth!

He had one hundred favourite foods!
Two hundred favourite hats!

And even though he was allergic...

he really liked cats!

It was worse in the street, among a large crowd,
where all the opinions seemed really loud.

So George raised two fingers right up to his ears
and pushed them in hard to block out his peers.

blah
BLAH
blah
blah
BLAH
blah
BLAH
blah
BLAH
BLAH
blah
blah
BLAH
blah
BLAH
blah
BLAH
blah
blah
BLAH
BLAH
blah
blah
blah
blah
BLAH
blah
blah
blah
BLAH
BLAH
BLAH
BLAH
blah
blah
BLAH
blah
blah

BLAH
BLAH
blah
BLAH
BLAH
BLAH
BLAH
BLAH
BLAH
blah
BLAH
blah
BLAH
blah
BLAH
blah
blah
...
BLAH
blah
BLAH
BLAH
blah
blah

BLAH BLAH BLAH

BLAH

BLAH

blah

blah

blah

blah

BLAH

blah

That's when he heard it –

a small, tiny sound...

a voice much quieter than the others around.

It didn't come from a mouth, it wasn't something said,
it seemed to be coming from inside his own head!

BLAH
blah
blah
blah
hello!
BLAH
BLAH
blah
blah
blah
blah
blah
BLAH

The voice told him nothing,
it just let him think,
and decide for himself
which he liked – blue or pink?

Having picked his favourite colour

he picked his favourite game.

He chose his favourite toy...

and liked his own name.

And George soon found out
when he didn't pretend
people saw the real him.
He made lots of new friends!

So now off George goes, ears sticking out wide,
leaving the other opinions behind.

He'll still always listen, but he might not agree.
"Only one person can make up my mind,
and that's..."

The end

for Natasha

x

Text and illustrations copyright © Felix Massie 2016

The right of Felix Massie to be identified as the author and illustrator
of this work has been asserted by him in accordance with the Copyright,
Designs and Patents Act, 1988 (United Kingdom).

First published in Great Britain in 2016 by Frances Lincoln Children's Books,
74-77 White Lion Street, London N1 9PF
www.franceslincoln.com

A catalogue record for this book is available from the British Library.

Hardback ISBN 978-1-84780-794-6
Paperback ISBN 978-1-84780-795-3

Illustrated digitally
Designed by Andrew Watson • Edited by Jenny Broom • Production by Laura Grandi

Printed in China
1 3 5 7 9 8 6 4 2

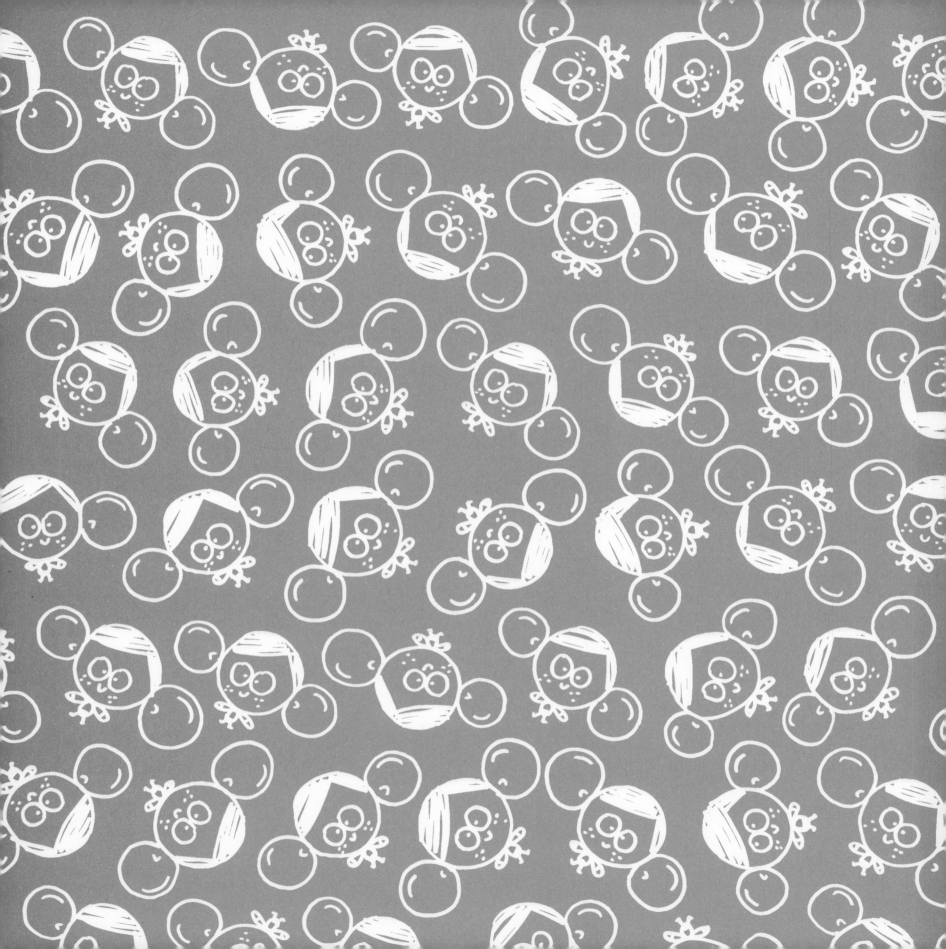